BY **Jerry Spinelli**

My Daddy and Me

ILLUSTRATED BY **Seymour Chwast**

Dragonfly Books  New York

To Nick and Patty

—J.S.

Dedicated to the memory of my daddy, Aaron L. Chwast

—S.C.

Published by
Dragonfly Books
an imprint of Random House Children's Books
a division of Random House, Inc.
New York

Visit us on the Web!
www.randomhouse.com/kids
Educators and librarians, for a variety of teaching tools, visit us at
www.randomhouse.com/teachers

Library of Congress Cataloging-in-Publication Data
Spinelli, Jerry.
My daddy and me / Jerry Spinelli ; illustrated by Seymour Chwast.
p. cm.
SUMMARY: A young boy describes the things he likes to do with his father, including making music, baking cookies, and fixing things.
ISBN-13: 978-0-375-80606-3 (hardcover) — ISBN-13: 978-0-375-90606-0 (lib. bdg.) —
ISBN-13: 978-0-553-11303-7 (pbk.)
ISBN-10: 0-375-80606-7 (hardcover) — ISBN-10: 0-375-90606-1 (lib. bdg.) —
ISBN-10: 0-553-11303-8 (pbk.)
[1. Fathers and sons—Fiction.] I. Chwast, Seymour, ill. II. Title.
PZ7.S75663 Dad 2003
[E]—dc21
2002009853

Reprinted by arrangement with Alfred A. Knopf Books for Young Readers
MANUFACTURED IN CHINA
First Dragonfly Books Edition
December 2006
10 9 8 7 6 5 4 3 2

I can't wait for my daddy
to come home from work.
There are so many things to do!

I sit at the window and when
I see him
I run outside.
He swings me onto his shoulders.
"Hey!" he calls to Mrs. Jones.
"Who's this cowpoke riding me?"

I run to the car.
"I want to drive!" I say.
"Okay, driver," he says,
"let's go to Kalamazoo."
I toot that horn and
turn that wheel
and that's just what
I do—
right there in the driveway—
I drive us to Kalamazoo!

Sometimes I don't run to greet him
at all.
I hide behind the sofa
or in a closet
or in the hamper.
But no matter where I hide,
he always
finds me.
How does Daddy do that?

I say to my daddy,
"What did you bring me?"
Sometimes he pulls out
an apple
or a toy
and sometimes he says,
"I brought you me!"

Daddy and I wrestle
on the living room rug.
I pin him.
"You're too strong for me,"
he says.

FLOUR

“Cookie time!” Daddy calls.
We make a mess in the kitchen.
We might make chocolate chip
or peanut butter,
but my favorites are
gingerbread men.

We plant tomatoes in the garden.
Daddy lets me dig the holes.
I'm good at that.
I'm good at eating too!

When the house breaks,
we have to fix it.
My job is to carry
the toolbox
and hand Daddy the hammer.
He says I'm his best helper.

Daddy gives me a haircut
in the bathroom.
It tickles.
Then I say, “Okay—my turn
to be the barber.”
But Daddy runs away!

My daddy should be a clown.
When he puts on his funny face,
it's like having my very own circus!
He walks like a penguin
and talks like a duck.
I pull on his nose
and tickle his toes—
and he does the same to me!

I'm Boy of the Day!
Daddy says we can go anywhere
I want.
Funny thing—even though I can go
anywhere I want,
the only place I really, really want to be is
right here
in Daddy's lap.

Daddy is teaching me to
stand on my head.
Pretty soon I'll be able
to do it
all by myself.

When we go for a walk,
we don't just walk—
we do fancy dance steps.
You'd think my dad had twenty kids!

We play magic.
I shake his hand and
his arm
falls off.
I turn around and
he's gone.
Then—*poof*—
he's back!

MAGIC
SHOW

Neighbors come to listen
when Daddy plays the harmonica
and I play
the drum.

Work makes Daddy tired.
Sometimes he's too tired to play tag
with me
or to stand up straight.
But never, ever is my daddy too tired
to sing me a lullaby
when it's time
for bed.

KERSHAW COUNTY LIBRARY
3 3255 00280 1547